For my Thisbe, who is everything beautiful…
*"There's no place in this whole entire world I'd rather be
than right here, with you."*
-Mama (L.S.)

To my courageous, tough, inspirational little Daddy's girl…
you keep me optimistic.
-Dada

To Thisbe, the inspiration for these images;
to Will and Emma, my inspirations every day.
-K.S.

Thisbe's *Promise*

First edition 2008

Library of Congress Control Number: 2008902877

Scott, Laurian
Thisbe's Promise/Laurian Scott; illustrated by Kelley Sharp

Summary: A mother shows her sick little girl the
world of promise that awaits outside her bedroom window.

ISBN-13: 978-0-9816642-0-0
ISBN-10: 0-9816642-0-2

1 2 3 4 5 6 7 8 9 10

Printed in China

The text is set in DeVinne BT.
The original paintings were done in watercolor on paper.
This book was designed by Shawn DuBard.

ETS Publishing
Franklin, Tennessee

Visit us at www.etspublishinghouse.com

Thisbe's *Promise*

Laurian Scott
Kelley Sharp

ETS
PUBLISHING

Thisbe had been in her bed
for a very, very long time.

But each day her mother would take her on distant
travels from the view outside her window,
just waiting for the day very soon when
Thisbe would step outside and see the world
once again for herself.

As a tiny seedling

floated past

Thisbe's window,

her mother said,

"Do you see that seedling, Thisbe?
That seedling was born
light as a feather.

Because it was *promised* the wind."

Just then, a butterfly flitted past,
landing lightly on a red flower.

"Do you see that beautiful butterfly?"
said Thisbe's mother.

"That butterfly was born
with crawling,
clinging feet.

Because it was
promised
a cocoon."

A hummingbird landed on a
nearby tree branch.
"Do you see that hummingbird?"
said Thisbe's mother.
"That hummingbird was born with wings.

Because it was *promised* the sky."

Thisbe's mother pointed to a fish swimming in the pond just beyond.

"Do you see that fish?"
said Thisbe's mother.

"That fish was born with gills.

Because it was *promised* the water."

Thisbe's mother pointed to a horse running
wild on a far hilltop.

"Do you see that horse?"
said Thisbe's mother.

"That horse was born with
strong,
whistling
legs.

Because it was *promised* the land."

Then, just on the horizon,
Thisbe's mother pointed to a starfish
on the seashore, clinging tightly
to a rock.

"Do you see that starfish?"
said Thisbe's mother.

"That starfish was born with
powerful
little
suckers.

Because it was *promised* the tide."

Past the horizon,
Thisbe's mother
pointed to an elephant
grazing on the tallest
treetop.

"Do you see that elephant?"
said Thisbe's mother.

"That elephant was born
with a long,
bending
trunk.

Because it was *promised* the trees. ”

And even still farther,

Thisbe's mother pointed to a great whale
diving
into
the
deep.

"Do you see that whale?"
said Thisbe's mother.

"That whale was born with a
gigantic tail.

Because it was *promised* the ocean."

Then, Thisbe's mother

kissed her sweet daughter's cheek and said,

"You see, Thisbe, you were born with a prayer.

Because you were *promised* the world...

And I was born with love in my heart.

Because I was *promised* you."

You are my wind,
  And I am your light as a feather.

You are my cocoon,
  And I am your crawling,
      clinging feet.

You are my sky,
  And I am your wings.

You are my water,
  And I am your gills.

You are my land,
  And I am your strong,
      whistling legs.

You are my tide,
And I am your little suckers.

You are my tree,
And I am your long,
bending trunk.

You are my ocean,
And I am your tail.

Then, one morning
Thisbe
started to feel stronger,

and as she was gazing at the horse
running wild on the hilltop
she said,

"I'm ready, Mama."

And *together*
they walked...

past Thisbe's
window,

Past the wind, past the flower, the tree, the pond, the hilltop, the horizon...

A portion of the proceeds from this book will go to aid the mission of
The Olive Branch Fund: A Thisbe and Noah Scott Legacy.

Please visit www.theolivebranchfund.org for more information.